love dealer

First published in Great Britain in 2024
by
Lyrical Messenger

Illustrations by Catriona Messenger
Cover Design by Lyrical Messenger
Formatting by Lyrical Messenger

ISBN: 978-1-7384443-0-4

First Edition

love dealer

Poetry, Illustrations and
Short Stories
by
Catriona Messenger

Love

With thanks to Love,
it feels good to trust you...

Find your own news

Where is life's rich tapestry
In the news we are fed
Why settle for fractional
When that is all that's being sold
Represented and impressed
But only part of the whole
Constantly repeated
Weighting a narrow view
Of a much richer story
The multitudes of existence
That are not represented
That could inspire balance
Uplift and motivate
Rather than the limited picture
Which divides and despairs
Anger and apathy
Leaking into our lives
Widen the aperture
Create your own portfolio
From the whole works
Of humanity
Find your own news

Drink

drink love like water
wear love like shoes
carry love like feathers
drink love to quench
wear love for comfort
carry love to grow light
and strong

The divine feminine

sitting well with the earth beneath us
waiting well for the *IS* to move us
moving well with the bodies around us
touching well hearts and minds
gently pressing well for expansive stretch
holding well and steady this sacred growth
lay down well past and future for presence
welcoming with humble grace
the whispers and silence in us
unconditional *Love* for us

April by the river Petteril

You sit still for a while
On this fallen tree
Changing its purpose
You rest and intend to listen
For the music

The symphony that surrounds you
What is written within these scores
The breeze dances past your ears
Gathering easy whirlwinds
Then dispersing

Brushing your shoulders
Lifting stresses as it goes
And collapsing them
Amongst the dry grasses - creaking
Last year's weeds, next year's soil

The pheasants crawk
Between the blackbird's trill
And the willow warbler's cascade
You hear distant canisters
Containing humans

Traversing the blue sky
On the ground the farmer
Levelling clots and ruts
In distant fields
As wary deer watch

Then retreat into woods
Did you hear their swift, delicate hooves
The Petteril calls
As water buffets over stones
White air-filled torrents

Move across the surface
Like smoke crackling from fires
Releasing melodies
Early Bumbles rumble
Should you be out yet

You ask as your dog snorts
In the undergrowth
The sound of discovering smells
And what more you exclaim…
As you let go, you wonder
If you could listen intimately enough
Might you…hear…the grass grow

Joy

Joy is a sphere
That holds everything
You can allow it to touch you
As it holds you
At the same time
As feeling anything
And everything else

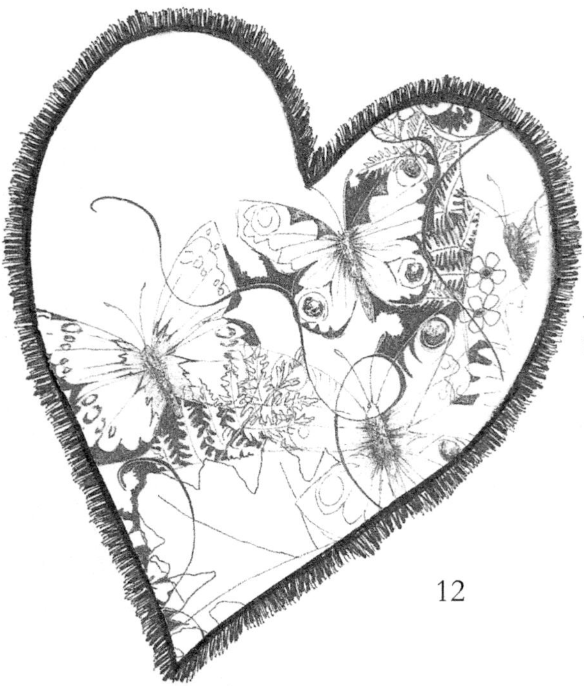

Tough

If we look at another
and think
I wouldn't want to be you
their path is tough
and they deserve our respect.

Overlapping

We don't end
at the edge
of our skin
we overlap
and influence
and are
overlapped
and influenced
which repeats
and repeats
beyond skin
beyond us
beyond
reaching as far
as our minds
can imagine
we are not small
because we exist
past ourselves
create past ourselves
move past ourselves

we are not powerless
we are powerful
we overlap
and influence
and are overlapped
and influenced
what do we want
to do
with this power?

Strength

Wake me up red
My wild woman
Energising this passion
With fire
And effortless courage
To be fully human
In front of all humanity
Stand up
Respect my full self
My freedom
My individuation
From the world
That brought me up
But is not me
Risking my uniqueness
Within our oneness
Facing wounds
And demons
Harnessing the beast inside
Working its anger
It’s fear, it’s shame – daringly
Saying No to fierce destruction
And Yes to fierce Love

For all awareness of life
Fully alive expressive life
Moment to moment
Embracing
Actualising – expanding
Seeking truth – living it
Maturing delight of challenge
Holding with grace my wild woman
Divine madness – wake up red

Overlooked

Often the people who are overlooked,
have the most important things to say!

Brave Soul

My loss is subversive
It undermines me
My perceived power
Taken down
Shattering established systems
Freeing me from false authority

My shocking dreadful loss
Wreaking havoc
Dissolving stubborn beliefs
Blasting out mortar
Crumbling my walls
Ready to rebuild

My life cannot evolve
Without something feral
Real change happens
With chaos and anger
You brought me to the ground
For repair and remodel

Loss is integral
Part of life
With the purpose of Gain
It Gifts New Life
Death is Courageous
Brave Soul

Clarity

The brilliance
of Anger
of Shame
of Forgiveness
all communication
the former are present
when truth is obscured
the latter is present
when truth is seen
All are presents
of Clarity

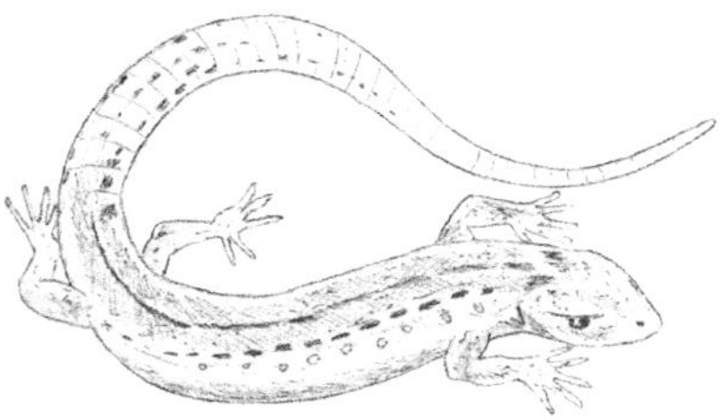

Diamonds

We seem to start with the dark: it seems to make sense that this is the problem. Our hidden parts must all be ugly: full of our fears, rich with wrong and shouldn't and not welcome; the cause of turmoil, unease and woes.

We rake around bringing up the past, reconciling perceived trauma and judgement of what's gone wrong. Reliving and adding creations of what's bad. What we need to change about ourselves. Aha moments of clarity? But never truly feeling much difference, or at least not for long, before we realise, we're still repeating life in the same way. Could we be looking elsewhere?

What if we started with the light? What if that's the only thing we are really scared of, the only thing we are hiding from, and the cause of all our turmoil? What if our most hidden parts are our talents and strengths and shiny parts? What if drilling into the dark rock is a nonsense, a distraction? The diamonds were mined for us before we were born; we already have them. Perhaps we could try wearing them?

Everyone

Either see love in everyone
Or barely see love in anyone…

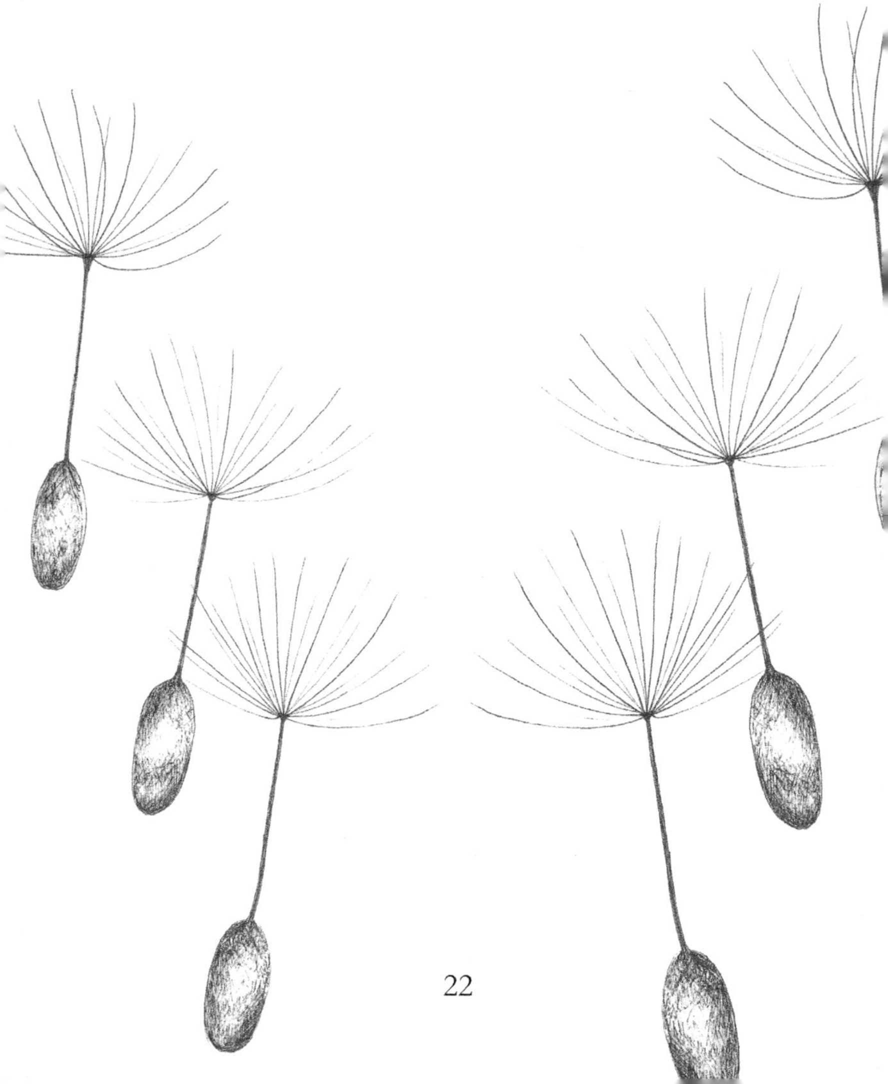

Hmm

I don't want to recover
I want to discover
I don't want to heal what was
I want to embrace what is
I want to live in the world
Like only this moment exists
Go everywhere
Do all things
Expecting nothing
Knowing nothing
Receiving everything
And giving it all away

Maturing

What if
growing
maturing
evolving
means
acceptance
that life
is not
about us
we are not
in control
and
we will die
-
does that feel
like
fear and anger
perceiving loss
of individual self
or
relief and release
and free-falling
into Oneness

Oh sleep

you are my dearest friend
I adore to spend the night
embraced in your dark
blanket of rest
together we reset
undo and lust for nothing
across a still landscape
our dreams can dance
their whispers or shouts drift
above the depths and slackening
the great loll of repose
why do you not join me
tonight, I shall surely
not unravel without you
the day unprocessed
will tighten and bind
I'll toss, turn and yearn
restless for you
my night-life love

Ok

Oh…
Ok
this
is
what
I'm
doing
now…

Resilience

And when a storm comes
our ideas of life come undone
the story we thought
undeniable
    how resilient will we be

What when the paths we walk
completely change
not what we expected
or imagined
    how resilient will we be

Is it dreamlike to believe
all we have and want is ours
at least the same or more
and if not
    how resilient will we be

When everything changes
and change everything always does
how different our surroundings will look
what can support
    how resilient **we** will be

Myself

the only limitations

are the ones

I

make for

myself

It is you in the mirror

There is a knock on your door
And you feel uneasy
But you do not answer your unease
You answer the door
There stands an odd creature
You try to work it out
But cannot
It's such a mixed up being
You struggle to make sense of it
The creature asks to come in
You look more closely
Squint your eyes
Ah, it looks like Expectations
So, you welcome it through your door
Invite it into your living room
Please make yourself at home
You say
I will boil the kettle
I will make you tea
Give you a biscuit
And enjoy your company
You pass by the mirror

En route to the kettle
Your reflection reminds you
You feel uneasy
But you like your guest
So, you look away
The house seems to be filled
With colour
And laughter
And purpose
The kettle whistles
The tea spoons clink
The biscuits crunch
What brings you here
You ask your guest
You, is the creature's response
Your unease flutters
But you are enjoying the ambience
Of Expectations
You push the truth away
The creature has a carpet bag
You watch as it is opened
And delight as lovely things are drawn out
Flowers more beautiful and sweeter
Than you thought possible
Works of art to adorn your walls
Music, jewels, futures
Brighter than you could imagine
Rugs for your hearth and your door
Porcelain for your cupboards

Silver for the drawers
And perfumes for your bathroom
Locks for your windows
Chains for your garden gate
Alarms for your porch
Bricks to build walls
Netting for camouflage
Armour for your loved ones
Weapons for your hands
Earplugs for your ears
Blinkers for your eyes
Turrets for your roof
Drawbridge for your drive
Suddenly you feel heavy
Pressed down
Closed in
Worried
Panicked even
Let me make you another cup of tea
Falls from your mouth
You pass by the mirror
En route to the kettle
Your reflection looks distant
Faded and unfamiliar
You do not like looking at it
So, you don't
The kettle whistles
The tea cups are too special to use
And you worry the creature

Will steal your silver away
You stand with your hands on the worktop
Unable to move
You want the creature to leave
But the locks and bricks and alarms
Make it too hard
The creature has morphed
Into your furniture
Across your floor
It's unsettling the cat
And distressing the dog
Your family's constrained
By chains
Your unease becomes ill
And you take to your bed
But, there is the creature on your pillows
Under the duvet
I want you to leave
You cry
Look at me it says
But the creature is hard to look at
And you pull the duvet over your head
Then ask for a cup of tea
The creature obliges
And passes by the mirror
En route to the kettle
You recognise the reflection
It is you in the mirror

See

The darkest corner
Is filled with light
Your eyes cannot see

Grace

when I welcome Grace
and natural can flow
Life *is* a benediction
constantly bestowed
pure and boundless treasures
the goodness of love will show
in unlimited presence
in Universal breath
…Breathe it in
it is the air we breathe - We need
notice, and breathe…
when Grace is welcomed
we are exposed, vulnerable
opened and swayed
by *all* of life
Grace's Golden brush
holding sadness and tenderness
sore and sensitive emptiness
All sweet miracles of existence
discovered with touch
Grace disappears us
reappears us
with an empty, full heart
fear, death, what is done
what needs to be done

All held, complete, in trust
Supreme with dignity
Grace is a law
simple – upright – direct
courage of the warrior
…to bow their head low
and come home…
Grace brings us hither
inward, outward together
lovingly aligning essence
Brilliance in body
In – can – des - cent
Grace is absolute – Love

The

seeing

is

the

doing

See

Red Campions

I found life in the red campions
Life refracted by my eyes
Their breezy swing and sway
Their delicate rubicund lives

Roots nuzzled into stillness
Surrounded by supportive leaves
Dainty heads reaching up for haze
Conversing with the chattering bees

They dance in these eyes
Like the curls around my face
The campions stir with grace
With movement there must be faith

Clouds roll along above
Though they are not in my view
Their interaction with the sun
Changes the campions hue

Their miraculous perfect petals
Speak to what's wise in me
Can I cherish my soil, my leaves
My delicate rubicund self
Can I sway and dance in the breeze

The therapy room of right

You go there
thinking something is rong
bits missing
or too many bits
life in bits
too many sharps and flats in your song
searching for something
to make you wright
to heal the rongness
if you're really listening
really seeing
you'll leave knowing
your rong is wrong
and you are **all-right**

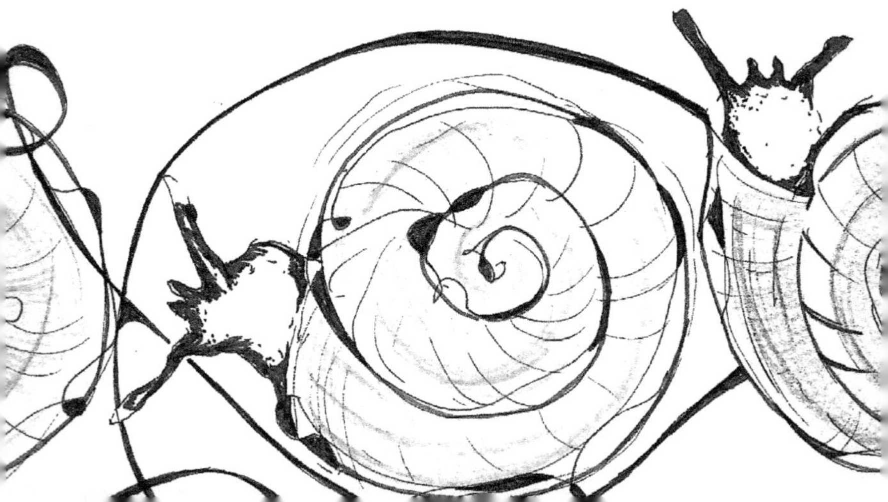

Unwanted

If I cannot change
reality
this does not
render me
powerless
My power
is choosing
how
I respond
to reality

The Workshop

I might not look like much from the outside, but inside there is a beautiful world; a fascinating terrain of life lived and tools gathered. Multi-layered, learning and growing, shelves filled with solutions and gifts to help me travel along my path.

My Dad's workshop did not look like much from the outside; a humble building cobbled together with metal and wood panels and a flat corrugated roof. But inside there was everything. Behind the metal door, which as a child once slammed across my fingers – this memory still makes me wince. Beyond the door, when I entered the workshop, it would occur to my eight-year-old self that no matter what the weather outside – hot as it could be on a summer's day – wild as it could be in autumn – inside the workshop always felt comfortable and safe.

I especially enjoyed visiting when the workshop was empty. No screeching circular saw threatening to take fingers. No welding sparks, sizzling and glowing with a drifting stench that hits your nose. No clashing hammer and whirl of wood-chewing drill. Good job my Dad learnt to use his tools well.

I enjoy that thought: using our tools well. I also remember that even when the workshop was empty there was a gentle, mysterious hum from the cylindrical lights for company.

I loved to tinker in this generous space. Ruffling in the sawdust rug to find discarded wood and opening oily dust clad boxes filled with treasure. My eyes would cast about in awe of myriad things waiting to be useful; and myriad tools, waiting to make use of things.

With hammer and nails, I would turn offcut pieces of wood into works of art, leaving them in pride of place on the workbench.

Now here I am in a different time and place; I am no longer eight, but if I look at my feet on the floor I can still see the sawdust rug. I can still feel the steady workshop inside myself. Myriad tools and useful things. Every nook and cranny of me filled up waiting to create; waiting to make and mend. Waiting to produce solutions and gifting years of gathered wisdom.

From the outside I might not look like much, but like my Dad's workshop, inside there is everything.

We Make

The sounds we make
They can land on the floor
They can float through the door
They can ring in ears
They can induce tears

I want

I want to commune in the silent language of all
Rather than these spoken words which fall
I want to lay with the meditative stillness of trees
Rather than running with time, trying to please
I want to watch the river with its steadfast flow
Rather than driving the motorway with its choking glow
I want to nurture with kindness a flexible home
Rather than rigid and critical, thick walls of stone
I want to love and honour even the tiniest form
Rather than cultivating discrimination normalising scorn
I want to gaze at my darkness with love in my heart
Rather than punishing myself for my imperfect parts
I want to be with each moment as each moment arrives
And be astonished by the stories that make all these lives

Elusive

Is oneness elusive
Or right under our noses
The soil supporting our feet
The community in our street
In our heartbroken grief
The air in our lungs
The letters in our songs
The tears in our eyes
The wind in our skies
Our truths and our lies
The thoughts in our minds
The treasures we find
The sleep in our beds
The words unsaid
Imaginings in our heads
The pictures of our dreams
The blood in our seams
Is oneness elusive

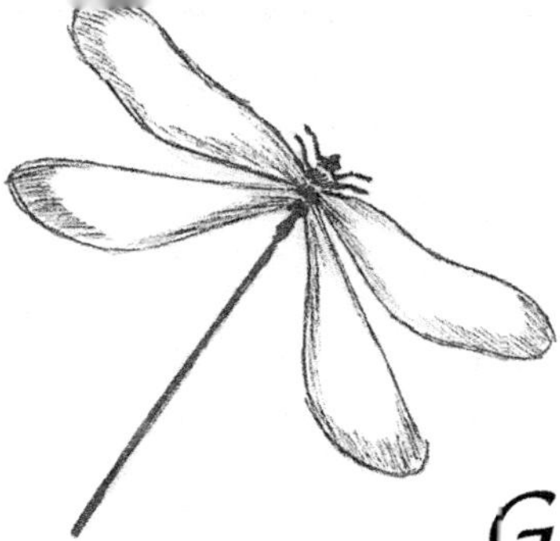

Gently

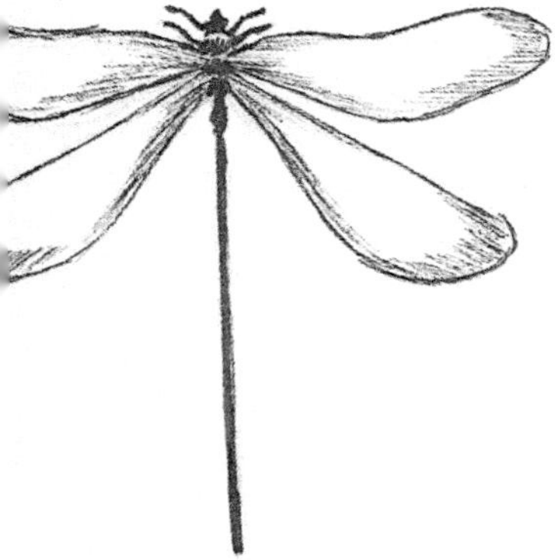

when
we hold
it all gently
there is room
for Love

lightly
experience
lightly
think
lightly
feel

move
change
heal

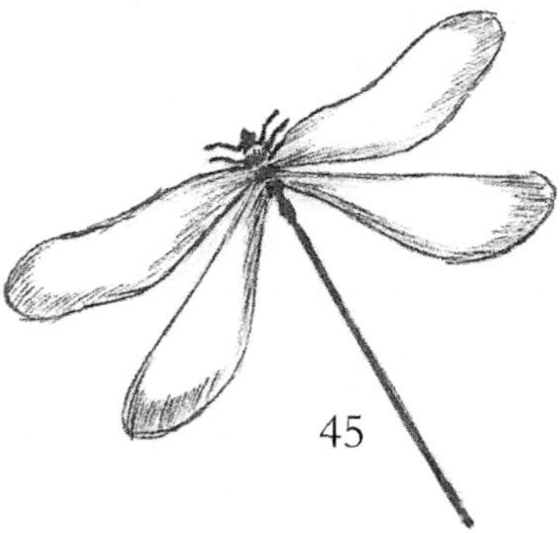

My Roots

I can stand rooted
in my belief
that this world
and that we
are beautiful
it exists
in us All and All things
it does pour out
over waterfalls
abundantly
washing us
soaking us
in its tremendously Gentle
ever-giving Love
regardless of old expectations
of how life looks
regardless of that which denies beauty
I no longer agree
to deny
the beautiful world
which exists in reach
if we want it – look for it
I do want a beautiful world
and finally, I see – really see
I can root myself
around this waterfall

of beautiful
changing expectations
to marrying Love
journeying with Love
exploring with Love
accepting Love
expecting Love
Love is beautiful
it's mine and it's yours
I will no longer deny it
here I am in this beautiful world
choosing to meet
in waterfalls of who we really are
that is where you will find me
might you wish to be soaked

of thinking

absurdity …

the

Explore

Thinking

I Woke

Having gone to bed still reeling and processing the stirred-up memories of physical trauma, I woke; although, had I been asleep? I was not sure, but there was a jolt: a strange pull from my mind. Was I teetering on the edge of consciousness? On the edge of oblivion? I noticed I wasn't breathing; the rise and fall of my chest was missing. With no sense of air entering and leaving my body, there was a still and empty feeling in my ribs. Am I dead, am I dead? A terrible unease overcame and sunk about me, accompanied by a hanging confusion and lurking just next to that; something like fear. I thought to sit up, then stand up; stepping away from the bed and turning. I made ready to see my body laying lifeless under the sheets. But I was not there. Still with uneasy confusion, I checked for my pulse. I could not find it; I checked all the usual places. And still there was no breath entering and leaving. Stillness.

I went to the bathroom expecting to find no reflection in the mirror, but there I was reflecting back at myself. How am I here, when I am sure I am dead?

And still no pulse. Still no breath. Still.

I thought to pick up my phone; I wanted to speak to someone, to hear if I could be heard. Am I still alive?

It was 11.45pm; was it too late, was anyone awake?

No one was. Death is lonely.

Fuck it

Let us start with No
Fuck it – fuck it all
All absurd inheritance
No more bending
Compromising
Adjusting
Deadening
Set the inheritance free
Just be – must be
It does not make sense
Even though sense
Could be made of it
No sense in it Now
Just be – must be
Has - to be
It is the only sense
I see
Fuck it – fuck it all
All I inherited
Now to honour and express
All that is just me
That is what I want
That is what I am offering
Just be -me

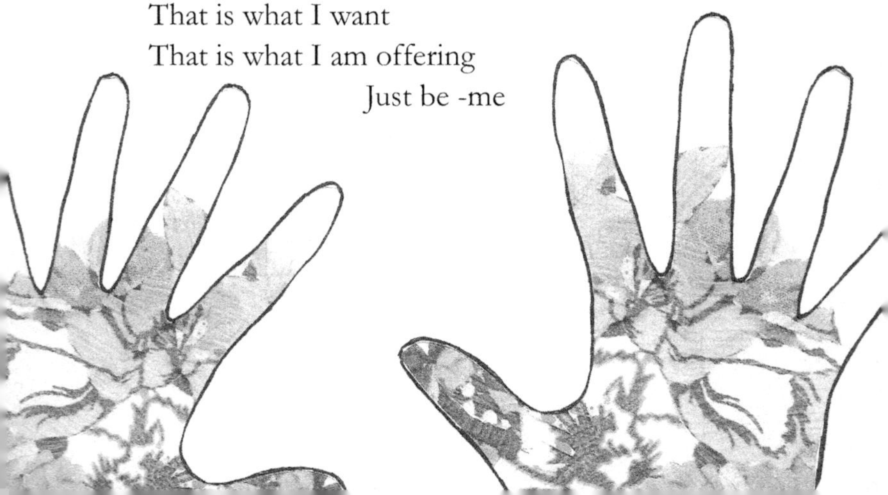

What if

What if life isn't a problem to solve

What if life is an experience to live

What if we never let go of awe and wonder

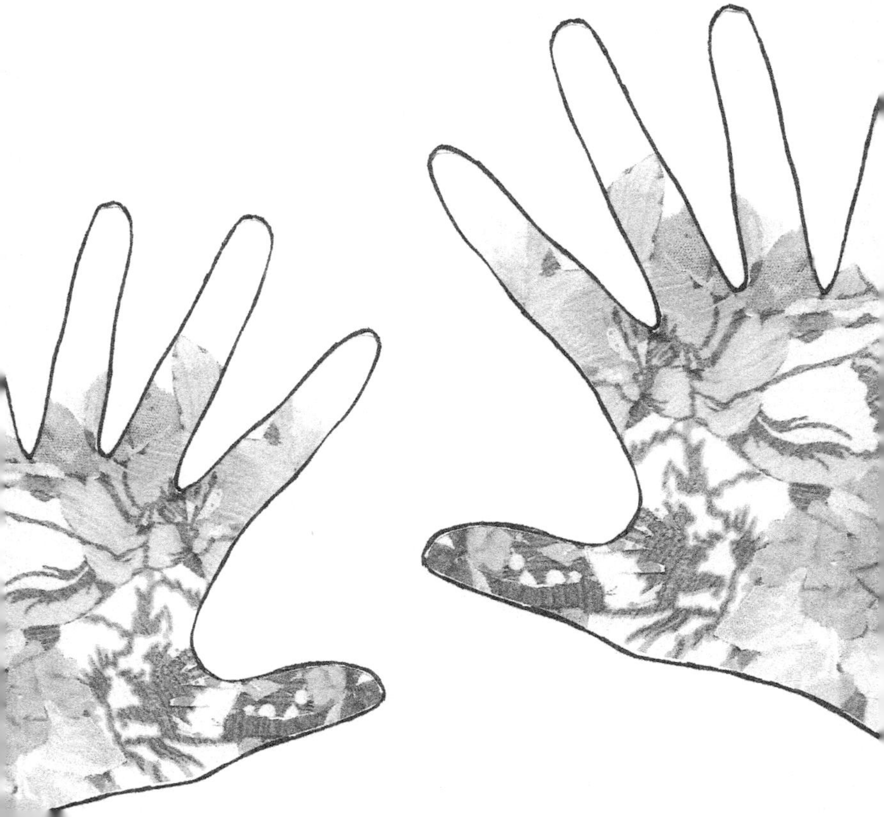

In Sync

Pain and Growth
Always in Sync

Lonely

loneliness
is
disconnection
and
disconnection
is avoidance

The banister

When you walk through the door
Hang up your coat
Take off your shoes
Steady yourself
Hand on the banister
Looking at the floor
Who am I
Where am I
Why
And emotional pain
Feels like physical pain
The banister is losing you
You drop to your knees
Face in hands
Sinking to the floor
And you give in
Open the gates
To a thousand years
Of strain
Tears and tears and tears
Surrender

Tension

Where are you
I know you are residing
Inside my dark places
Between tissues, sinew
Wrapping up bones tightly
Changing soft into hard
And distorting my stance
Lurking in layers of cells
Dampening natural flow
Flood waters that gathered debris
As the waters receded
Sticks, stones, disrupted life
Got stuck between my teeth
In my joints, my connective edges
Building up tension – gathered blockages
So, let me see you - find you - know you
To start clearing the paths, the courses
I'll pull out the sticks and make a fire
I'll pick up the stones and make a path
I'll write you letters and songs
Creating treasures
With all that was disrupted
My body can be soft
My flow can be free
Of tension

We fear

When we judge there is another will
When we judge there is only one way
When we judge there is not enough
When we judge there is no love
When we judge that we have lost
When we judge that we have failed
When we judge that we are wrong
When we judge that they are wrong
When we judge there is no freedom
When we judge we are alone
When we judge there is no meaning
When we judge
When we judge
When we judge
We fear

Anger

I want to expand
I want to burn hot
With determination
And courage
I want life to freely flow
In me
Through me
From me
I want to be a beacon
For Love
I want to be a voice
For Love
It's mine
And always has been
Show it - expand it
And so, it is
Amen

Wordless Empathy

And the elephant
it entered the room
with her, it was unruly
awkward and cumbersome
An elephant not sitting well
in its own momentous skin
Sundered, uneasy, weary
taking up lots of space
and therefore pushing
against everyone's comfort
All in the room were
making choices
how to react, respond, ignore
this big grey lump
that comes along with her
And sadly
because it is an elephant
avoidance manifested
as the collective choice
Ah but not for one, someone
did want something more
to acknowledge
rather than ignore

An inner exploration
was occurring within the scene
How to acknowledge
how to love this weighty
broken creature
When it was time to depart
acknowledgment came
from one brave soul
love was their goal
Their gift came
with briny filled eyes
ache filled faces
and a physical embrace
hoping to impart
some strength
Then with one more offering
a silent significant nod
all wordless empathy
Her elephant felt embraced
seen, and loved
It was not set free
the hole of brokenness
was deep
but she felt less lonely
in this moment of love
Love accepted
with tender gratitude

Wisdom

What we want
And what we need
Are two
Different things

Change

Changing the words
Changes the story
Changes the speaker
Changes the listener
Changes the outcome

A Violence

We three received
Unbearable, unthinkable
Violence

Raking at high speed
Heavy unruly land rover
As we ambled, Oblivious
Across the road

I'm sure we'd be
Thinking thoughts
Of lucky contentment
To have family days
And a delightful home
We were all but
In reach of

Never
Could have imagined
Such a brutal act
Befalling us
Violating
Our soft bodies

Snapped neck
Broken, shattered bones
Ruptured flesh and arteries
Collapsing lung
Bleeding brain

How do we recover
When one of us did not…

How do we recover
From this
Physical cataclysm
How do we recover
From experiencing
The worst
Our worst
Of what could happen

How do we recover?

All Life

There is so much Life in Death
Too much not to be lived in
And no I don't know
All the *life* it is
But I feel it advancing
Making space in my cells
Travelling outrageously beyond my blood
Sleepless bed
Golden thread
Waking up with freedom
Giving it no meaning
Feeling beyond feelings
Something irresistible without identity
There is so much Life in Death
Waking me up to be lived in
Spilling Love
Unconditional Drug
Detoxing dreaming
The sky without ceiling
I have an inkling of the life it is
Original feeling beyond feelings
Before misperceived meaning
Here Real comes
Love has won
There is so much Life in Death
Life that wants to be lived in

All the way along the river

It was middling March, but it was colder than she had expected, which was disappointing; she had presumed there would be more warmth. The landscape seemed dark and bleak, but she was sure that really it was not. She lay down, resting and looking more closely, listening more closely; she merged with her surroundings. Yes, she could hear it, feel it; life flowing in this place. Life that was rich with stories. Many of them did not feel so good. There was something called sadness. It was everywhere. So, she looked more closely and listened more closely, felt more closely: there was more than sadness; there were many other things to be discovered.

She was near the source of the river, its sound delighted her; it sang beautifully and to follow it was her heart's desire. Her legs felt wobbly, but that would pass. They would get stronger and look after her while she looked for treasures. The air felt fresh as it travelled up her nose and into her lungs; she warmed it there, then let it go, ready for another breath, which it seemed just magically happened.

The ground was lumpy and bumpy under her feet; covered with wild grass, but soft. She wondered what might be seen below this tangle of yellow tuftiness. Were there precious things, other worlds with unusual and unknown creatures? She decided to place her feet with care. Her legs were stronger moment by moment and so was curiosity. The gentle flow of the river was a golden thread laid across the landscape. It disappeared beyond what her eyes could perceive; all she knew at this moment was it felt right to follow it.

The river had bends and wiggles; nothing was straight. She saw a sandy patch that had gathered in a turn; a good place to explore. As she walked and her feet sank into the sand, it felt cold between her toes. Noticing how interesting these foot shaped trenches were, she sat down. Poking her fingers into the sand, enjoying how it felt – gritty, moist, mouldable. She drew patterns that echoed the sound of the water around her imprinted feet, making more shapes and adding embellishments: little pebbles, grass and tiny flowers that were growing right at the edge of the bank. They had sweet little faces full of joy. They perfectly complimented her creative sandy expression. Time for refreshments. Washing her hands in the water and drying them on her clothes, she had a drink and found some cheese sandwiches in her knapsack. Contentedly she ate, enjoying the different textures and tastes of the bread and cheese. She also watched and listened and merged with the music of life. There was a slight vibration on the ground which was increasing: thud, clod, thud – another traveller on their way, wanting to cross the river and wearing big heavy boots.

They stepped onto the sandy patch, crushing her creativity, leapt over the river, and continued on their way! Unpleasant feelings gathered. Her perception that her creation did not matter, was not honoured, or cared for, hurt. She lifted the squashed flowers and pebbles out of the sand and washed them in the river; leaving them hidden, at the edge, tucked under the bank where they would be safe from other big heavy boots. But that felt odd, to hide these beautiful things, so she sat down again and recreated her sandy creation around the footprints of the traveller's big boots.

Time to walk on; but before she started, she watched this other traveller, far off in the distance, striding away heading for something, she couldn't see what. They were pulling and adjusting their knapsack; it looked heavy. She picked hers up and appreciated how light it was. Although the other traveller seemed focused and sure about their path, she decided to keep following the river, because it felt like her home: listening to it, looking at it and feeling it, felt good.

Birds flitted about above and sometimes they landed on rocks. One bobbed up and down and so she copied this movement, enjoying a silent conversation with this silky feathered friend. She noticed that silence was not empty, but full; filled with something that felt generous and powerful. She thought it was love. The sky was turning blue above, as grey flossy clouds began to evaporate. She looked up at the expanse of blue and shouted 'How beautiful you are,' with her arms reaching out to embrace the sky! There were birds high up in the air, creating patterns with their flight.

She could hear their calls of joy in agreement. Trees were showing up in the landscape now and along the water's edge. They appeared in multiple shapes and stature. Leaves were beginning to grow on the branches. It felt like an invitation to climb up high and see her world from a different view. She was feeling strong and picked a tall tree with many branches. The tree was happy to greet her and honoured to offer her a different perspective. 'Trees are good' she thought, as she caressed the rough bark with her soft fingers. It smelled green with life and sweet with sappy blood. She navigated the branches trying to coordinate four limbs, feeling a little apprehension about leaving the steady ground. Six branches up, she stopped. It had caught her attention how different her world felt being as tall as a tree. She was sharing its gentle strength, and wisdom gained over more years than she could imagine. Because of that her world looked safer, brighter, and more inviting. 'I appreciate you' she whispered through the bark into the tree's rings. She imagined her words echoing through its layers of wood and landing in the trees heart, wherever that was. Quietly she stayed held by this tree, just looking at the world until she felt sleepy.

Climbing down she found a seat amongst some roots closer to the water; just close enough to dip in her toes. The sun was bright now; it warmed her skin. She found it interesting to feel how the temperature of the water on her toes was in comparison to the heated air and how holding her feet in the water cooled the blood travelling up her legs. There was also a gentle breeze by the water. She sat very still, enjoying how it felt on her face while listening to the susurration of the leaves in the trees. Sounding like a music, she felt she had invented this place as she looked closely and listened closely and fell into its rhythm. It smelt green and mellow; the air tasted like blossom and honey and the sounds were a lullaby. Rest was hers and she drifted off to sleep, her head gently held by a tree's root.

On waking up she stayed still for a moment appreciating the tree roots holding her and the sun keeping her warm. How I love sleep and being held: these were her thoughts. Her ears listened to the discourse of the river and wondered about its history. She felt hunger again, but looking in her knapsack there was nothing else to eat. 'Hmm, I would really like something to eat.' She stood up, stretched, and started to meander along the edge of the river. Meandering became more like clambering as the banks became higher and more rugged. Her stomach became more demanding in its want for food and she noticed her pace was slowing as she was thinking longingly about her earlier cheese sandwich. She did not know how or where to find something to eat. She sat on the edge of a rock and said to the river 'What should I do? How can I help myself?' She was sure that the river did have a mouth somewhere and the answer would come. She became aware someone was busy behind her. She turned around and said 'Hello.' The traveller jumped. 'Oh, I hadn't noticed you there.' 'I'm hungry' she exclaimed to this traveller. 'I'm busy,' said the other traveller who was picking berries; 'I haven't got time to waste, I'm in a hurry!' they added to their reply!

'Can you eat those berries?' she asked. 'Of course,' said the traveller 'What a stupid question.' Laughing, they went on their way. She did not like the feelings that gathered around her; thoughts that she was stupid. She picked some berries for herself and sat back down to ponder: if someone does not know something, is that stupid? And the answer, she heard inside herself was No. 'I knew these feelings were telling me something wasn't true.' As she enjoyed the berries, she intended to listen to herself some more.

There was a world inside her that was fantastic and interesting. It seemed more lucid, more free, more autonomous, than the physical world. She could not choose where the river went but she could choose what to do in each moment, and the thoughts that she wanted to think…

I see you

I wish you to feel free
In your summer dress
On a crisp almost autumnal day
I see you

I see you - frees you
I see you - tells you
It's good to be you

As you collect your frogs
You show them your love
And I see you

Be ok

I want to be
uncomfortable
in the world
and for that
to be ok

Choose

How about calling out
Love and honour
Make that more
Give that more
Normalise
Love and honour

Rather than calling out
Fear and dishonour
Make this less
Diminish it
Disappear it
Replace it

Putting our attention on
Love and honour

Exchange

It's not death, it's exchange
It's not loss, it's merging
It's not an end, it's continuation

Nothing is destroyed or created
It's all recycling and flowing
All the same stuff in different shapes

One thing moving, as all possibilities
Presenting in all possible ways
It's not death, it's exchange

God - up

Something to believe in?
so many meanings - perceptions
God communicates
speaking to our inner world
what do I believe
around this word – God
that which already holds me
and that which I wish to hold
I believe in the God of wisdom
the God of inner strength
the God of gentle tenderness
kindness and boundless love
I believe in the God holding presence
and the God holding me
the God holding you
that even in the most terrible
desperate and frightening times
there is God, tailoring the details
to whatever carries you through
building you up, raising us up
up and up, the God of up
that's the God I can
in this moment perceive
and believe in

NO

the reaction

Let me start with NO, the smallest of words
with the biggest heart. Fuck it all -
wretched world, with such a passion for fear.
For self-preservation and brother and sister annihilation.
A passion for validation over authenticity
and passion for control destroying freedom.
Creating the caged, weary, resentful
and the caged, enraged,
hate-filled, spiteful.
Ones that strive for success over justice
and greed over equality.
Desiring exclusion
to keep these concepts set in stone and safe.
Lest we change and must wear someone else's shoes!
Surely, we die if we take down our walls: NO,
we are already dead under the weight of them.

An invitation to goodness

the response
By Miriam Ruth Lowe

Come beautiful world with such potential
for love
Come those who rise in justice and soar with
healing in their wings
Come those who stop to shoulder the weight of
those unseen
Come free of heart and generous of hand
And generous of heart and free of hand
Come friend called honour you are
welcome here
Come all who cry there is room enough
Come try on my shoes and let me slip on yours
Come open doors and wide, wild spaces
That we may roam and build a place that we
might call home

I fall

I fall
in Love
a dozen times
a day
– more even
it is medicine – Love
it opens
peels
reveals
all that is exquisite
real, and surreal
in Love
all that appears
not good
falls like crumbling plaster
from walls
that
have
stood
too long
so many times
I fall
in Love
each day

Emptying

Many
little
deaths
on
the
way
to
dying

Man made

The current human condition in a 'plastic bag'
Man made it, put it together
Mixed it up in a capitalist's crock
A concoction of 'needs met'
We carry our 'stuff' in you
Hauling it around with us
Buying into ever more 'stuff'
All on the outside of us
Overloaded and manufactured
Distracting us from our disconnection
Disconnected from ourselves
And the natural world
From that of substance
From the earth and our own Grace
Disintegrated as we are
You and the 'stuff' we carry in you
Has infiltrated our natural world
And our inner world
Contaminating all that is good
You are corroded, but deathless…
'Unmet needs'
This 'plastic bag' disease
Has infiltrated us
Should we now look inside ourselves?
Should we now reconnect to nature?
To clean up our disintegration from Grace

My works

I am a work
of my inner world
always
communicating
watch myself
listen to myself
my words
my responses
and actions
it's all
communicating

Me!

Oneness and separation

Oneness looks at their reflection
In a shimmering pool
And sees separation
Separation listens to their echo
In a bright blue sky
And hears oneness

You do not Matter?

What a choice to live with
- not Mattering
You feel irrelevant and worthless
the cause of problems
the cause of pain
what a truth to believe in
what a burden to carry
and what a signal to give out
for life to respond to
you believe
you're not deserving
pointless, unknown
valueless
wretched even
if you do not Matter
must you be
less than
nothing
invisible
unwanted
the whole world Matters
but for some reason
- you do not?

Why?
how can that be?
have you been bad
do you hurt others
do you not belong
here or anywhere
no voice
no needs
they're not allowed
this cannot be true
everyone matters
so you must too!
No to not mattering
'No!'
this is not a truth
this is perception gone wrong
a cognitive mistake
search your inner worlds
for Love
for Mattering
unfold and unravel
reveal
caught between, but seeing
truth
creating healing
the old neural pathways
sewn in youth
are ready for unpicking
fraying at the edges for change

and just when you think
you're stitching with Gold
life brings you challenge
and here you are
vulnerable, floundering
in old pathways
but the new roads
have been started
you can continue building
blowing away the fog
you know who you are
you recognise the old story
these childhood choices
can still sneak in

but you see them and let go
saying 'No!'
because you now know
you Matter…

With Gold

I sleep
I heal
In the morning
I wake
I remember
And my heart breaks

I sleep
I heal
In the morning
I wake
I remember
My broken heart
With one stitch of Gold

I sleep
I heal
In the morning
I wake
I remember
My broken heart
With two stitches of Gold

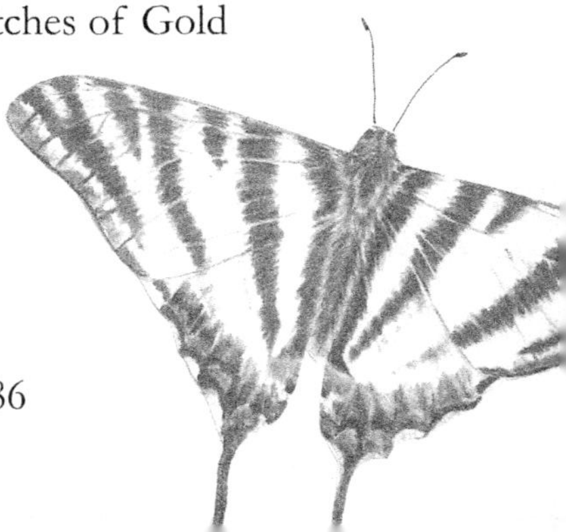

I sleep
I heal
In the morning
I wake
I remember
And my heart
Is more beautiful
Stitched with Gold

The mistaken you

Loyalty misunderstood
The only betrayal
That is real
Is the betrayal
Of self

Any other betrayal
Is a work of fiction
That ties us in
To a story
Of false safety

To give over to
Is not giving at all
It only takes away
From both
No one triumphs

And when this
Is brought home
Seen in your living room
It comes with regret
Then mourning

Who am I
What was lost
Inside you still
Patiently waiting
Your faithful return

The real you

A voice with love

As she lays with this man
And he sings his poetry
Letters making words
Words that have his hands

His hands caress her wounds
We all have them
This man has a gift of deep and gentle touch
Mending scars from cutting up life

He reached inside himself, and asked
All letters carefully resourced from love
They heal as she feels their mirror on her
Seeing her vulnerable yet dynamic truths

Moving shifting her pains
Each letter bringing resolve
To her most beautiful self
Generously rediscovering alive

Yes, she had asked to be heard
To be seen and given to
She knew; she knew; she was
Beautiful; in an equally beautiful world

And calling hearts *are* heard
This man remembered himself
And sings the gifts of his poetry
And she lays with him and listens

Making love with letters
Love letters in our hands
Playing our part, the healing of hearts
With our words *we can*
Bring an abundance of Love

Silent truth

If I want to speak of reality,
silence is a great place to start

Shine

Diamonds
in my body,
diamonds
in my mind

A trap?

Is an identity a trap
Limiting to one way
One story
With walls
And narrow focus
Creating safety
Or neurosis?

Betrayal

The worst thing I could do
To you
You needed loyalty
And I needed you

I clipped my wings
I betrayed myself
And that's what we do
For survival

Done with thinking

My head is exhausted
Thinking feels futile
Trying to understand
The unknowable
What are my thoughts achieving
What do they even mean
Or change
Beyond
My emotional response
Only adding overwhelm

It's all going to unfold
With or without them

Lower them down
Bring them down
Watch them fall
Sinking, transforming
Into useable fuel
As I let them move
Towards my faithful rhythm
Quell them in my heart
My true intelligence

Silenced head
Trusting essence
All I need know
Exists inside me
Shh
Listen
To the whisperings
Of steady Miracles
The lullaby
Of All is Ok

My Love
And wrapped
In Gold

Freedom

What is it, to me
Moment to moment living
Not doing because it has always been done
Not doing because they are doing it
Doing from inspiration of spirit
Which asks for growth but never harms
No slavery to empty ideas and concepts
Freedom to change this mind
Rather than following the ruts
Awareness of the merry-go-round
The ability to step off
And look for something else
Listening for and following alive
Regardless of fear
That prefers familiar routes
And safety barriers
Freedom to live life
Like it does not even exist
Filling cells with heart
Freedom is not selfish
Freedom travels with grace
Because it does not belong to one
It connects us and delights us
Synthesising desires to collaborate
Building newly imagined worlds
And being open to more…

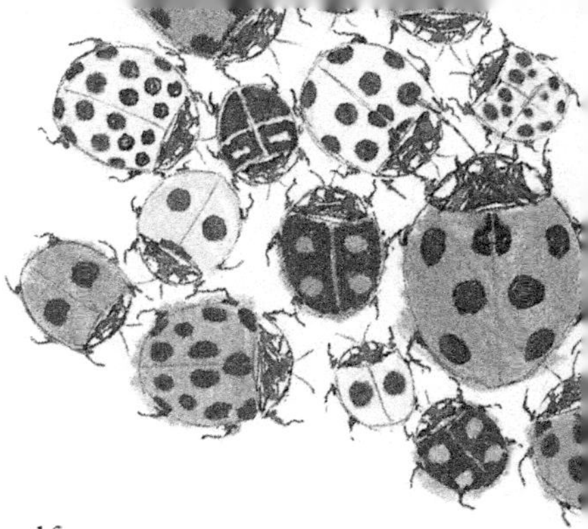

And… perhaps this is in itself
An idea and a concept
And therefore, freedom does not exist
Only the idea of it exists
Oh…well…
This is an idea of freedom

God

never stops me
only I stop me
and what will
happen if I say
yes as openly
as God as
sure as
God
as
receptive
responsive and
welcoming as God

Heaven

could we each

be our own angel

and could

we make

this world

our heaven

Answers

In
quietness
all
things
are
answered

Kali

Invited or not Kali will come
It feels too hard having beliefs destroyed
Our self is so invested in them
Our lives so enmeshed with them
To destroy our perceived reality
That's hard, cataclysmic even
Having constructs in place
Feels safe and secure
Justified and defended
Take our perceived world away
And we will be exposed and vulnerable
Ruined, empty, lost – found - open – free!?
Invited or not Kali will come

My fool

I sing the heavens across these skies
It’s always love I have in mind
Creating fools to be my muse
To inspire all this love for you

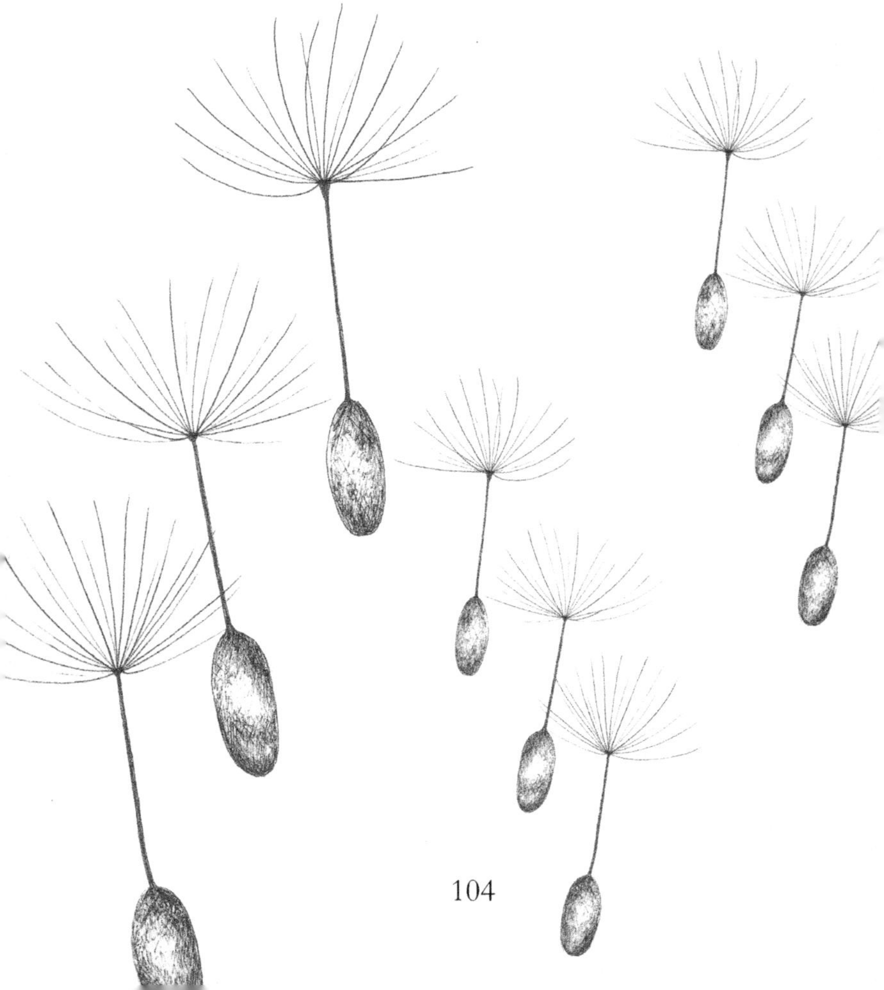

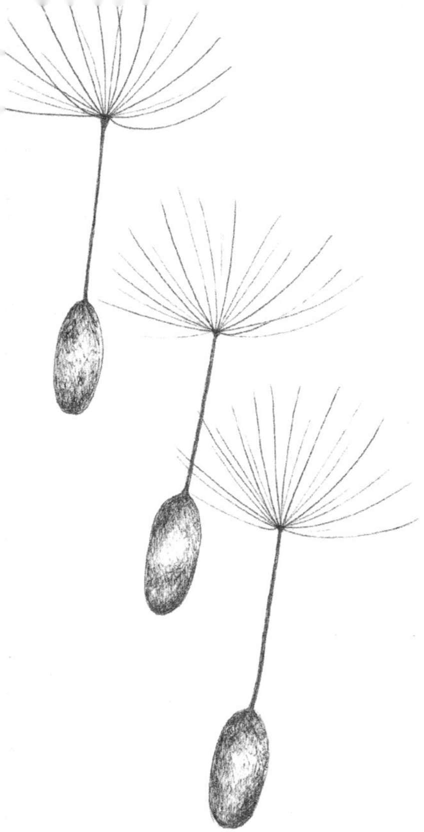

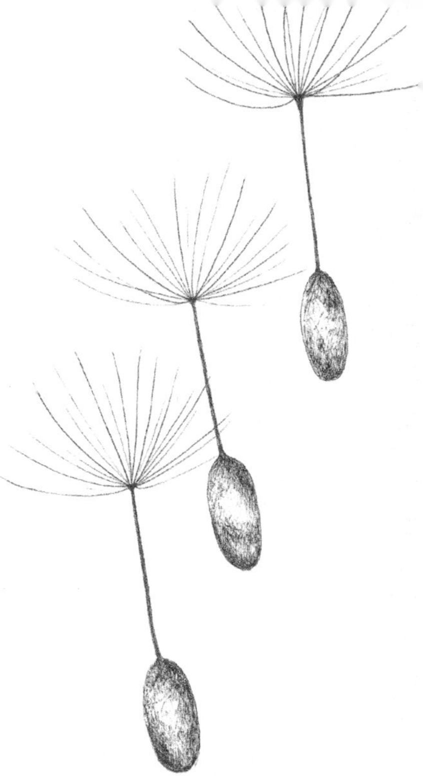

Paying attention

There it is
That which is trying to love us
Everywhere
Are we paying attention?

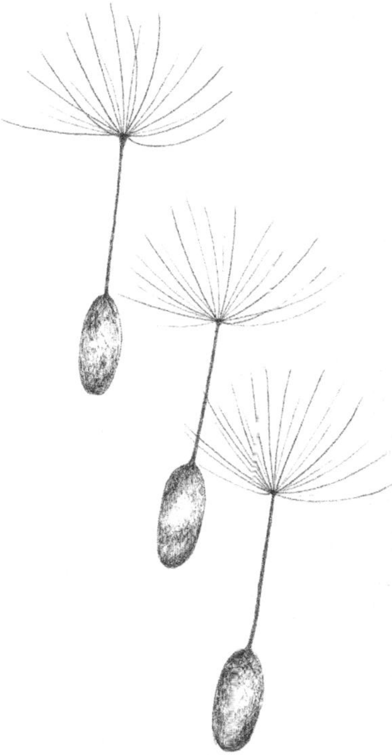

Seriously

And what happens, when we look down
we see our own feet
planted on this ground
how do they sit
how do they travel
on this earth
look at them
weighted by us
governed by us
moved by us
bound
by the paths in our mind
leaving their imprint
with each step
treading, trampling
trudging
tracking
Stamp!
Seriously
how do we want them to be
the imprints of our feet
heavy – unruly - bias
narrow
crass, thoughtless
reckless, self-centred
ungracious

are our paths ill-considered
senseless
undiscerning
irreflective
short-sighted

Seriously

what could our imprint be
how could we govern our feet
could we be unified in our steps
aware, heedful, canny
concerned, cooperative
earnestly interested
awake and honest
sincere
participating
with strength, and with tenderness
with all the gifts in between
our footwear could be
honour and grace
foot – falling - love
for all feet and the ground underneath

Seriously

The challenge

I challenge you
to be free with me
to embrace
without fear
all of me
my dear
not to steer
me
to your places
to your story
of limited love
this is how it is
you'll say
and I will want
to turn away
life can be
anything
it wants to be
through me
always love
never wrong
I can't tolerate
another
fragmented song

Others agendas

When the world looks different
In your spirited beautiful eyes
When your response seems odd
To the majority
In your brilliant beautiful heart
You're paving the way

You may be finding it hard
Seeing the world this way
Running opposed to societal narratives
I want you to embrace who you are
Change is inevitable and starts
With the smallest different view

Embraced and nurtured
You don't have to understand
You will not know the ultimate outcome
It's beyond your time
Your purpose is simple
Easy – it is simply being and embracing you

The taxi

You wait at the pole
The empty taxi pole
Pockets of life's noises
Drifting in and out
And here's your stance
You and your whole life
Standing – waiting - wondering
A blurry mix of everything
Joining together in this moment
Of you, at a pole
You – what even is that
You enquire
Who really are we
Really – truly – surely
It's something more simple
Underneath these years
The memories
Are they even real
The roles you've played
The players you've walked with
The stories stitching it all
Here's the taxi
And if you choose awareness
You'll hear your 'old car' judgements
Your 'untidy car' judgements
Your 'big hippy' judgements

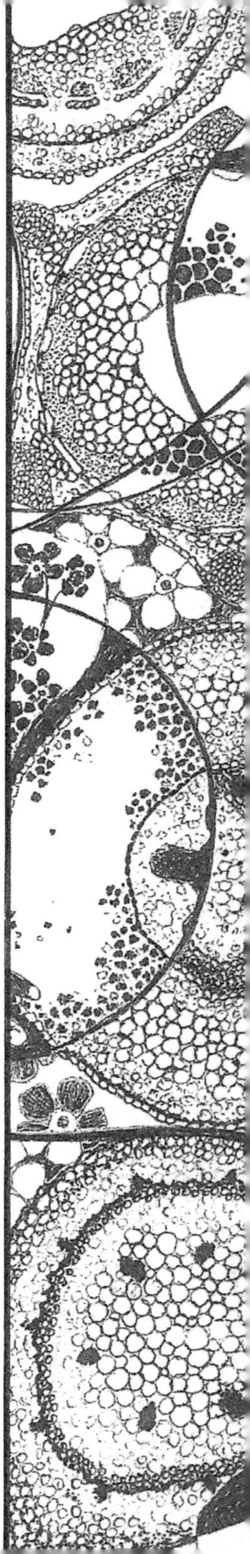

And the, ‘oh, nice aura’ judgements
Judgements, judgements
Judgements
In the way of
Simply who we are
The conversation flows
Your unspoken enquiry
Still hanging in the air
This taxi man announces
‘We are all here to look after each other’
‘I think the world has forgotten that’
You reply
‘Yes, it can seem that way’ he says
Ah – silence – thoughts
We’re all here to look after each other
Underneath the questions and judgements
The answers are waiting and simple
Really – truly - surely
Simple

Always Loved

"Look at me bear! Strong and powerful behind these bars, where I put you." Marcus was kicking the bars.
"Look at me bear!"

"I…", he announced, turning his back on the cage: "… am free. You can't touch me." He spun back around to look at the defeated animal, picking up his rifle which was leaning against the outside wall of this forgotten place, where no one comes except Marcus and now a groggy, wounded bear. Holding his gun at the bars he traced the creature as it paced back and forth…

Marcus' world went dark. For in this moment old painful pictures of suffering flowed through his head, rendering his body stiff. The gun stood still. He saw himself on the floor in the cold, with a chain round his ankle; the same chain that now lay coiled in his pocket. His father loomed over his fear-filled body demanding to know if he was strong and ready to fight or a weak, useless coward? He remembered being goaded, beaten, and left in the dark to consider this question. A vivid image of his father's fist coming towards his face played out. The gun dropped from his hands, clattering on the rocky ground, and bringing Marcus back to where he was now: full of hate, deep pain, feeling abandoned and alone; grotesquely desperate to express his bloody, tangled self.

"I'm gonna kill you bear", he threatened loudly. "You should suffer because you're pathetic; you're fuckin nothin' and I can kill you!"

Every day Marcus came and shot his rifle into the bear; not killing the creature but causing it to suffer. Marcus kicked the bars, leaned into them and bellowed air from his lungs trying to release his own wounds; never feeling better, consumed as he was with his own grief.

The bear rammed and leaned into the bars, also bellowing air from its lungs. Its suffering and angry fear matched Marcus' and when he caught the animal's eyes, he saw things he did not want to. These moments of connection showed him his own pain and he would quickly turn away, struggling with his truth.

The day quickly came that Marcus found the bear dead. He felt overcome with loss! He shot his rifle many times into the dead animal, the word No ascending through him "NO NO fuckin NO!"

Dropping to the floor he kneeled with his forehead on the ground, howling into the earth beneath him; overwhelmed by this life. He yearned to feel something else, something that would take it all away. This consumed his whole body.

~~~~~~~~~~~~~~~~~~~~~~~~~~~~~~~~~~~~~~

The day Marcus found the bear dead was the day Mhairi found her son. She'd been directed into the forest reluctantly by some people in the town. With difficulty she had followed a long, overgrown, uneven track and had come across this figure of a man ahead of her. She held back, peering from behind a tree as she wondered what was happening. This was just the moment when Marcus repeatedly shot his rifle at the dead bear and dropped to the ground screaming. Mhairi was frightened by what she was witnessing. What was happening!? Was this her son!? The fear she was feeling was shrieking within her and as tears of painful distress fell down her cheeks, she ran. Fast as she could she ran past trees; colliding with them, tripping over the uneven, plant woven ground. She felt desperate to be away from this scene that shook her.

Marcus heard a sound of someone in the forest; it startled him out of his pain. It filled him with adrenalin. He needed to know who had seen him; he turned on his feet and gave chase. This was his world, amongst the trees. He easily closed the gap between him and this figure crashing through ahead of him. With his gun on his back, he negotiated the uneven ground with ease and quickly caught his prey.

Mhairi was deeply aware he pursued her; the fear inside her went electric and her body gave in to her fate. As Marcus jumped her to the ground, the depths of Mhairi's lungs screeched, "I'm your Mother!"
~~~~~~~~~~~~~~~~~~~~~~~~~~~~~~~~~~~~~~

Marcus heard her words, but they had little impact on him. On top of Mhairi, he pulled his gun round into her face.

"WHO ARE YOU?" he yelled.

"YOUR MOTHER!" Mhairi hollered back to him.

"WHO ARE YOU?" yelled a snarling Marcus again.

Mhairi's fear started to fall as she looked in Marcus' eyes and saw his fear, his pain and, behind that, she saw her son.

"I'm Mhairi and you are my son."

The words, 'My Son' reverberated through Marcus and it knocked him off kilter. Still on top of this woman, gun in her face, his confusion besieged him.
"What, WHAT? Fuck you, bitch. Do you want me to pull the trigger?" he said as he stood up but still held the gun in Mhairi's face.

~~~~~~~~~~~~~~~~~~~~~~~~~~~~~~~~~~

There was great pain in Mhairi; the fact that she didn't try to leave all those years ago had eaten away at her being and forbidden her any rest. She had wanted to leave, but stayed to protect her child. She knew Max had plans for their son and there was no way he would let her leave with Marcus' hand in hers.
~~~~~~~~~~~~~~~~~~~~~~~~~~~~~~~~~~

The last day that Mhairi spent with Marcus was his seventh birthday. There were no friends to invite and no family, just the two of them with a shop bought cake and a small present. Mother and son; one desperately unhappy and scared, the other just wanting to be a child in a house filled with anger, fear, and sadness.

Mhairi remembers Max coming through the front door, with all the indications she needed to send Marcus to his room. He was not drunk, he looked straight through them as if they did not exist. Quiet and sober was not good, it meant something deeply profound was gathering inside him, like lava heating and expanding until the tension breaks through the rocky surface. Her next moment was a fury of enraged fists and then regaining her consciousness on the living room floor. Groggy and in pain, hardly able to see at all, she looked for her son, but she was alone.

Mhairi surrendered; she had nothing left: no fight, no reason to live. Was she ready to die?

She lay down and gave in. Was this it? No more manipulation, no more brutal behaviour? But it wasn't the end she had been longing for: there was no relief. The only love she had ever known, her baby boy, was gone.

Whispering from her lips was, "I can't do this, I just need to die, I just want to die, please let me die." Mhairi lay on the floor, but she could not die, her son was with a monster. She could not turn away from that.

~~~~~~~~~~~~~~~~~~~~~~~~~~~~~~~~~~~~

Marcus could not understand what to do with all that was eating away at the depths of him. There was a hole inside him, a hole of blackness that sucked everything into it and swirled round like a whirlpool. He felt sick when he looked at it.

At 14 he stood inside a ring of men; another 14-year-old boy stood across from him. He could hear his father behind him, "You better not let me down son, you better beat the hell out of him!"

Marcus felt alone and empty, and time slowed down. The hectic noise of the voracious crowd, all wanting their bets to pay off, diminished into nothingness. Looking into the eyes of this boy in front of him, the blood racing through his veins with adrenalin… calmed.

The noise of his settling heartbeat became hypnotic. He saw himself in this other boy: hurting, scared, desperate. Marcus closed his eyes.

Wham!

The other boy had taken his opportunity. Marcus fell to the floor; the blow had so taken him by surprise. As he lay there, time sped up again. The crowd noise returned to full volume, his heart raced and so again did adrenalin. He felt a sudden heat of fear in him; fear of what it meant to lose.
~~~~~~~~~~~~~~~~~~~~~~~~~~~~~~~~~~~~

Fuelled by this heat which was laced with anger, he leapt up and protected himself by beating this wretched boy in front of him. Marcus lost all sense of what he was doing and ultimately had to be pulled off a bleeding, broken 14-year-old who was dragged away.

Marcus was surrounded by the grotesque cheers of those holding winning bets. Relief washed over him; he would be left alone tonight. He held in tears; his relief was deeply filled with emotional pain.

Later he was allowed to go to his room while his father and other revellers drank, laughed and gloated. Marcus lay in his sparse room, hands swollen and throbbing. He waited in a long comfortless stillness until the noise ceased. Then knowing they had drunk themselves unconscious, Marcus could cry. The salty tears stung the cut on his face where that boy had struck him, the only strike he was able to make. It stung. It hurt. It all hurt. He curled up and hoped that sleep would take it all away.

~~~~~~~~~~~~~~~~~~~~~~~~~~~~~~~~~~~

At 17, Marcus stood and watched as a bear attacked his father. His gun was pointed and he could hear his father cry out for him to shoot the bear. Marcus was frozen; he could not do it. All that his father had done to him violently raced through his mind, and he ran. He ran home, his heart beating out of his chest. Marcus did not know what to do when he got there, the intensity of his choice was
~~~~~~~~~~~~~~~~~~~~~~~~~~~~~~~~~~~

unbearable – overwhelming. He quickly tried to shut it out to survive, choosing to do things, get on with things that had to be done. Cutting wood, shooting, and fishing to eat, fixing anything and everything; but being alone hung gravely over Marcus as the next weeks unfolded. He was lost and utterly confused about who he was, what he had done and his life with his father. He did have relief, but he swung between that and fear, because he didn't actually know if his father was dead. Marcus spent the next couple of years by himself in this wilderness life; what else could he do, he knew only this way of being. He avoided that part of the forest that would confirm if his father had died. His actions were still haunting him; he could not face them.

~~~~~~~~~~~~~~~~~~~~~~~~~~~~~~~~~~~

Mhairi had not died the day that Max gave his final beating to her and took Marcus away. She recovered and never gave up hope of finding her son. She had to believe she could find him to forgive herself. Her determination brought her to him these many years later. She was a weak and frail lady; years of abuse had left her so.

This felt like her last opportunity; this small town on the edge of wilderness. Was this the place? Was Marcus going to be here? In this small town there was hope as much as there was fear. And so much guilt. Would Marcus hate her, thinking she had abandoned him? Would Max kill her? Would this strange man and boy, that no-one really wanted to talk about, really be her husband and son?
~~~~~~~~~~~~~~~~~~~~~~~~~~~~~~~~~~~

Back with her boy - who was now a man - pointing a gun at her, Mhairi exclaimed "I want to leave!"

Marcus stood back so she could get up. He watched this woman speedily walking away, still pointing his gun at her and telling her if she spoke to anyone about him, he would kill her. Terrible feelings were leaking inside him and he told himself to "Shut up!" He was sure he could hit her with a shot. Unable to admit he did not want to, he told himself she was now too far away.

Marcus did not know that Mhairi would come back and find him again. Her heart would not let her leave without speaking itself to him. Looking past her fears of what Marcus appeared to be was going to take much courage and be deeply painful for Mhairi. She knew she didn't have long; every day she was feeling weaker and needed to show her son that, no matter what, she loved him.

Mhairi found somewhere to stay and although she was struggling with her health she went back into the forest. It began to be clear that Max was not around, but she didn't dare ask. Marcus continued to be hostile at first, but she kept returning and gently asking to sit with him.

And so it was that with a little time Mhairi did sit next to Marcus, trying desperately to let go of her fear. The fear which told her that before her was a monster. The fear that told her to protect herself from him. The fear that told her to make judgment: of him; of herself; of the man that moulded him into this twisted and torn up human being. Her heart was telling her to keep trying, but fear spoke ardently over her of impossibilities and the need to leave. The agony of guilt held her responsible and at the same time offered her thoughts of no responsibility at all, to protect herself. "There is nothing I can do." span round in her mind. "There is nothing I can do."

Sitting next to Marcus with all this churning inside her, she lowered her head, its heaviness acutely painful. Mhairi's heart shouted louder and, in her mind, she prayed for help. "I want to show Marcus my love. Help me let go of my fear and know what I can do." Her right hand was on her lap gripped into a tight fist; it relaxed and fell open. She held it there and stretched it out. She knew it was an invitation; an invitation to Marcus, to love. She moved it towards him.

Marcus was seething beside her, rocking back and forth in his own torture; unaware of anything Mhairi was doing. Full of rage for this woman who dared to sit next to this monster that he was, he thought he might just kill her!

Opening his tightly squeezed eyes, he saw her open hand above his lap. He felt something run through his body like nothing he could ever remember feeling before. What was this strange feeling?

He felt safe.

Safe? There was a silent moment in him that rage was eager to consume. But his chained-up heart wanted love badly, so Marcus took Mhairi's open hand and gripped it. His body wrenched forward heavy blackness lurching out of him through his mouth as he vomited violently between his legs.

~~~~~~

Mhairi's visits continued and it became clear to Marcus she was not well.

The strange boy that no one wanted to talk about took his mother to the town's hospital. After what was a truly short time for Mother and Son to heal, Mhairi did not have long left in this world.

Marcus sat with his Mother – his Mother!

He knew Mhairi was drifting from him and Marcus did not want her to leave. He was mourning a lifetime with her he now longed to have. He did not remember any time before this with her, but perhaps it existed somewhere inside him.

In this short time together, Mhairi told Marcus she loved him every day. He thought he had never been told this before and it caused resentment and confusion in him. It stirred something else inside him too: a feeling that he could be loved; hard to hold on to, but in the depths somewhere this feeling lingered. Perhaps from his childhood it lived on; those forgotten memories of being told he was loved by his Mother. Was her love still stored inside him, waiting for her return to remind Marcus who he really was – he was love – deep inside?
~~~~~~

Under the damage, the abuse, the abandoned boy; not abandoned at all – Always Loved. Marcus looked at Mhairi and she was smiling at him. The terror of losing this woman who showed him part of himself that was previously lost felt unbearable. Mhairi began to speak and Marcus felt a glitch of warmth inside him; holding him. "Remember how much I love you. Find my love inside you and use it, Marcus, to love yourself."

Soon the strings were cut and Mhairi left this world.

"NO, NO, fuckin NO" flew from Marcus' mouth amongst spit and tears. He left the hospital in a rage of despair, punching walls and wildly venting at the staff as he left.

Marcus returned to the cabin in the forest. There was a dreadful feeling of disconnection from this place; a hatred of it and everything that had happened here. Night time soon came upon him. He gave in to rest, sitting outside with the trees, as the sky sunk away to be replaced by ink and stars.

"I am loved?" Marcus questioned, looking up at the night sky.

"That makes me feel angry" he told the stars as he noticed the burning sensation in his body. The intensity of his building rage began to overwhelm him; his fists tightened. He looked around desperate to find a way to release it. His hands leapt to his face, "NO NO fuckin NO" charged from his mouth, fingers digging into his own flesh. He released them, flinging his arms backwards.

He emptied out his pain with agonising volume up to the night sky. The stars heard and witnessed the might of his distress. When he got to the edge of his rage and despair, he opened his eyes. There were the stars still looking back at him.

Then came a moment of silence; a moment of stillness in Marcus. Just for a moment; just enough to start a connection to himself – to his own love.

Then Marcus reached into his pocket for that chain he had carried for so long. He threw it as far as he could, his head whipped forward to his knees. And he cried.
He cried and cried.

Beautiful souls

you fill yourselves up
and pour over your edges
you choose alive
choosing love

those you meet
feel honoured to know you
and heartbroken to lose you
such admiration for you

you fill yourselves up
and pour over your edges
you choose alive
choosing love

love is courageous
and there will be challenge
on this path you walk but
you will never be alone

Beautiful souls

Trapped emotion

You have already felt it
Yet it still shows up
In your body, through
Your mind, heavy
In your heart
Sickly in your gut
Because you hang on
Reluctant to be more...
You are not living
Who you are beyond it
Because you are scared
To be all you are beyond it...

Happy

I want you to shine brightly
I want you to be radiant
This is my voice
Not the one inside
That tells you
Your happiness takes something away
From someone else
Their comfort in their own lies
The voice, that belonged to someone else
Time to make these lies uncomfortable
Time to shine brightly
Because there is another voice
It speaks a different message
You are not meant to be like this
It says – you are meant to be brilliantly you
With lustre, you are joy, you are love
Boundless and radiant, a giver of gifts
I will reassure the voice of fear
It has no relevance to you now
You can be radiant and truly bold
With trust that being you
Was never wrong, more than ok
It is truly all for you
The you - which lives - in Happy

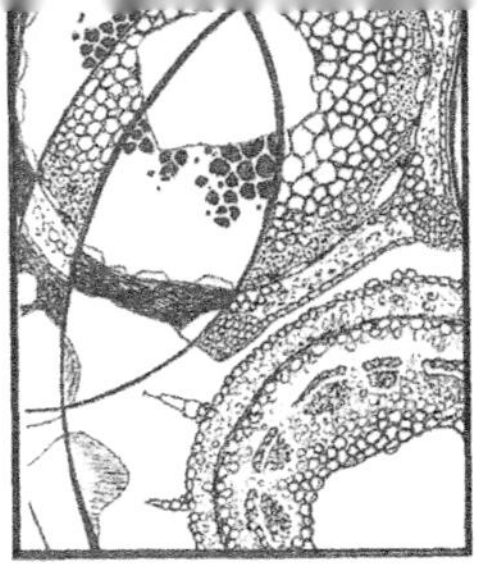

All

Anything that can exist,
will exist – always

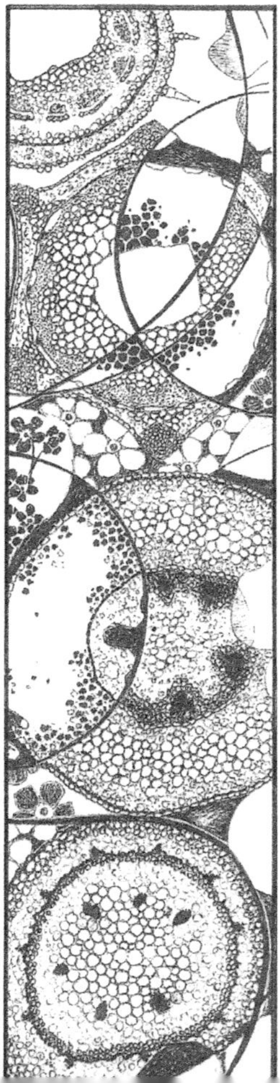

See

My
perspective
is the key
to My
experience

I want to speak in Love

I want to put down my pen
And open my mouth
I want to bring the dance
Outside
Let it breathe
Creating ease
I want to delight in being me
To trust the waves
That fill my sea
Walking the water
Of Love's decree

My God will help me
Simply because I ask
My God will guide me
In this beautiful task
Speaking Love

I want to trust
That my inside can live
This world outside of me
Be honoured
And thrive
I want to give

My gift of honour
To myself
Knowing all is safe
Because only Love
Is real and free
I'm in your hands
You're holding me

My God will help me
Simply because I ask
My God will guide me
In my beautiful task
Speaking Love

And being me
Is light and simple
And filled with Love
Even when I cannot see
I want to put down my pen
And open my mouth
I want to bring the dance
Outside
And breathe
With ease

You're all for me
I'm in your hands
Real and free
Speaking Love
With me

Oh, dearest one

Come in close with me
Put the world down
For a moment, Just let it be
Come in close
Listen with me
Find the voice inside
That wishes to be kind
Not the voice
Of narrow perception
The voice that deeply knows
Who you can really be
The depths you can discover
With your courageous heart
Including all the broken parts
Put this world down
For just a moment with me
Please just listen and hear
There is kind love for you
My dear, under surfaces
And superfluous voices

Real is softer and quieter
But freer and truer
Safe and secure
If you will stop and listen
Spend moments with me
Listen deeply and surely
Persistently loving – truly
Oh, dearest one
Come in close with me

What if...

what if I can't
maybe you can
what if I cannot do this
I think you are
What if the pain never goes
What if that's ok
What if I'm saying no
I'm listening
It's too hard, I'm too scarred
A work of art
A mess
Beautiful things are born from chaos
I do still see beauty
You want to
I do
Good for you
Can I hold it all
If you cannot I'll hold it for you
Hold me too
Always

See

You cannot
Change something
You do not see

Digestible

what you live you must digest
if you think it's too big,
too uncomfortable, seen as wretched
you might ignore it, avoid it
leaving it sitting heavy
it will start to rot, decay
the unpleasant smell
and taste will implore
your search to be rid
of such an unpalatable thing
looking for solutions
to cover it, drown it, dilute it
or somehow magic it away
what you live must be digested
inside you waiting for its exit
you're gonna have to feel it
moving through you
in all it weight and awkward shape
points and sharp edges
feel those wounds, abrasions
and inflammations

feeling it does digest it
it may be a challenge,
may take you to your bed
may mess with your heart and head
may hinder and blacken some days
but it will no longer be
rotting, heavy and undigested

Bring my whole self

The desire to do something good in the world
Appreciation of the love I feel and want to share
Aspiration to be the best I can be and inspire that in others
Sharing authentically my true experience
Knowing all the knowledge I need I have and sharing it
Connecting courageously from my secure self
Inspiring and delighting with enthusiasm and joy
Purposely fighting for everyone's well-being
Assuring others **All** that they are is beautiful

Oblivion

It seems when dynamic change
Wants us
It needs our willingness
To look into oblivion
Standing on the thin crumbling edge
Of an unknown, which warrants
Everything, to be a letting go
A gigantic free fall
With no idea, no concepts
Of future moments or outcomes
To courageously embrace the uncharted
As mere glimpses gradually unfold
Holding faith with our limited mind
Acknowledging the great emptiness
Ahead of us, yet seeing it
Full with more than we can comprehend
Our fears will spill out to be heard
Felt as chaos as we fall
Into the black hole of vital change
Oblivion

Courage

You have rage of the heart
Inside you – don't you?
The lion's roar
That places your hand on doors
And opens them

And you hear the fears
That rally around you – don't you?
Old stories sweating
Clipping your wings

But safe is small
Safe stays the same
Safe stays at home
Safe stays in doors
Strangling your courage
That wants to sing

You feel your rage of the heart within
Leading you to something new
New thoughts, actions
And Other worlds

'Scary,' say your old stories
'Yes,' says your heart-filled rage

And sure, you can falter
Wobble and be deceived
By stories keeping you safe
And small - bereaved

You have rage of the heart
Inside you – don't you?
You feel its power and tremor
Beginning to speak - and sing
Yet, fears will come in

Yes, you may stumble
But heart-filled rage will win
Because love is where
All and everything begins

Remember your courage
Rage of the heart
It's always yours
The lion's roar
Placing your hand on doors
Walking you through
To the bigger version of you

Love is where you began
And always you can - begin again
Rage of the heart is yours
Opening doors - the lion's roar

For the forever broken hearted

Every day you face your world
And yes, you face it broken-hearted
You said 'No' for as long as it felt you could
While you gently stitched yourself with Gold

You are no longer afraid of oblivion
You are simultaneously
Less tolerant and more compassionate
Of this perfectly imperfect world

You now walk against the desire to hide yourself away
You now choose to breathe into all your tension
And your first-hand knowledge of devastation
What else might you be asked to survive?

You explore the gifts your broken heart exposed
Aspects of you that went unnurtured

Forgotten in the corners of your cupboards
Spiders' webs had made them difficult to see

Life blew up and obliterated the dusty silk
All of you exposed, strewn across your upended floor
Where do you begin when you can feel it all
You begin by introducing yourself to pieces of yourself

But that is hard, it is all so terribly hard
And all simultaneously so utterly beautiful
You've become accustomed to feeling extremes
The world looks very different…but…
you did not want this

You *are* broken……can you even keep turning up?
You are asking, with longing, recurrent questions
And there are just… no answers
But… you notice you now care less for answers

As it all falls through the gaps of your brokenness anyway
Everything has become harder to hold
Life now runs through your fingers like oil

You were forced to let go of your greatest letting go

And somehow you know you are ok
Somehow broken is ok

And growth… always your asking
Did you understand… what you'd have to give up?
To be more whole......did you understand
The enormity of asking to be more?

Did you know growth comes with pain?
And…. here comes the agony of looking back
for another way
Another road to where you are now
Wanting a different story – hurts more

Multiple depths more than to hold this reality
More than saying ok to this unwanted, painful
Agonisingly upended path with no clear route
The person walking it…. *IS*…

More open, more brilliant, brighter, more generous,
Courageous, this forever broken-hearted you
Can and will traverse this courage you have for Love
You have more than ever to give

And now you give Love with *ALL* your stitches of Gold

It's time

Yes ain't it time
To be human
We think - we are
I'm human, but
Am I really
How human am I
In any given moment
Am I slumbered
Into easy ways
Well-worn channels
Of being less than
Hiding for fear
Of stepping out
And saying yes
Or saying no
This is not enough
This is disconnected
And a betrayal
To humanity
Shying away from
Interdependence
Masked by inflation
Or deflation
Warped and withered
Why are we less
And going along with it
Why do we lie to ourselves
Look at the clues to our
Hidden inhumanity

There in our daily movements
Our thoughts and actions
Judgments
Who are you judging right now
As more or less than
There it is
Inhumanity
It hides in us all
In our slumber
In our denial
Of interdependence
The world is growing
Yet how humanity shrinks
Let us wake up tomorrow
Shake up tomorrow
With compassion
Over our self-concern
With gratitude
Over our greed
With together
Over us and them
With same
Over discrimination
Honour over desire
Humility over pride
We need to be awake
To do this
We need to be open
To do this
We need to be honest
With ourselves - to do this

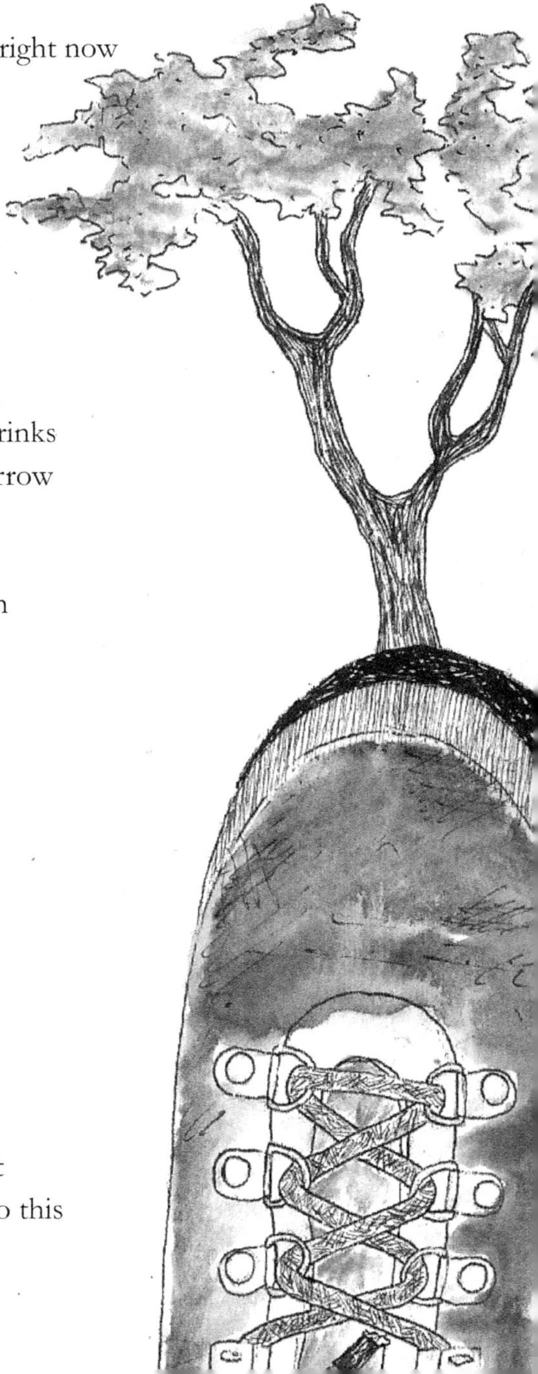

We need to see
Our own moments
Of inhumanity
To be more human
To mature
To bloom
To experience
The intrinsic joy
Of alive
Beyond a walking sleep
Accepting fully
Who we really are
Interdependent
Connected
Fully human

Making friends

Inside me resides the Devil
He dwells in my head
Holding me tightly
Cursing in my neural pathways
Like hot blood in my veins
Is he, my enemy?
Is he, my hate, my anger?
My unrelenting pain?
Does he flood me with sadness?
The yellow puss in my wounds
When I stumble, was it his foot?
And when I fall, did he push?
My shocking thoughts, his deluded mind?
His thirst for power over me
My harsh words
Did he plant them as seeds
And rub his hands
As they grew to fruition?
Does he play a merriful dance
Through my life with glee?
Or is he overwhelmed, exhausted
Feeling hopeless like me?
Who is this Devil that wreaks havoc in me?
I put out my hands, I am forlorn
I'm broken and blind, I want you to know
Can you see what you're doing?
Is this what you want?
To destroy your host
Filling my world with fear?
Taking any glint, any slip
Any hope of love?

I feel afraid and alone
I feel abandoned, I feel wrong.
I don't belong.
I don't make sense.
I'm not worthy, not loved.
The fear grows intense.
The Devil is me!
I am the Devil!
I deserve to die!
I'm wretched and useless
Revolting and bad!
The world hates me, I hate the world
It left me empty, when I needed to be filled
Left me cold, when I needed to be touched
Left me mute, when I needed to be heard
Was blind to me, when I needed to be seen
This devil is me!
I am my emptiness, I am my hurt
My suffering, my pain
I was love.
I am love.
I am my crying, aching, dying heart
Red with sores and bruises, bleeding
This is not how it's meant to be!
This devil, the world created in me.
There's a tremendous ache in him
Vibrating through and through
It aches too hard, I want to die!
I look at him, cascades of water,
Burst from his eyes
Jagged noise explodes from his mouth
My body falls and flails about
He's hurting in me and it hurts too much
I want him to go
I need him to leave

I'm You! He shouts, yells,
Hollers at me
I jerk out of crying - I Stop!
Silence falls over me, time stands still
He has my attention
What do you want?
Love, is his answer
I want love, I want love
I wanted love
All I wanted was love
It was not meant to be like this
He said on his knees
Hands together, praying on the floor
Looking lost, looking drained.
He looks exhausted to me.
I feel scared, confused, anxious and alone
I expected love to be my home
I am red with anger and grotesque with fear
All I needed was somebody to hear
I want to be full, warm, cradled and heard
I want to matter, be known and feel loved
I would have felt safe
I would have blossomed
And healthily grown
No flailing around, desperate to be known
No fear – filled choices and desperate ideas
Who I was, would have felt easy and clear
Love, is how it is meant to be
There is so much time for you to love me
We are all full of the devil of pain
Hear our true feelings and heal our way
Talk to me, hear my heart
No judgment, No blame

This, a new start, you, and me
Find compassion for each other
This devil and me
With a kind listening ear
We can work through fear
Love is waiting, it's our birth-right
Healing brokenness and putting this right
Love is a rainbow of all that feels good
Of course, love is the answer
We would all love if we could
So, listen to that devil, as he shows us his pain
Soothe him, love him
Love me, knowing
Love is how it is meant to be.

Explore

Question our minds
Change the stories we serve
Create a different world

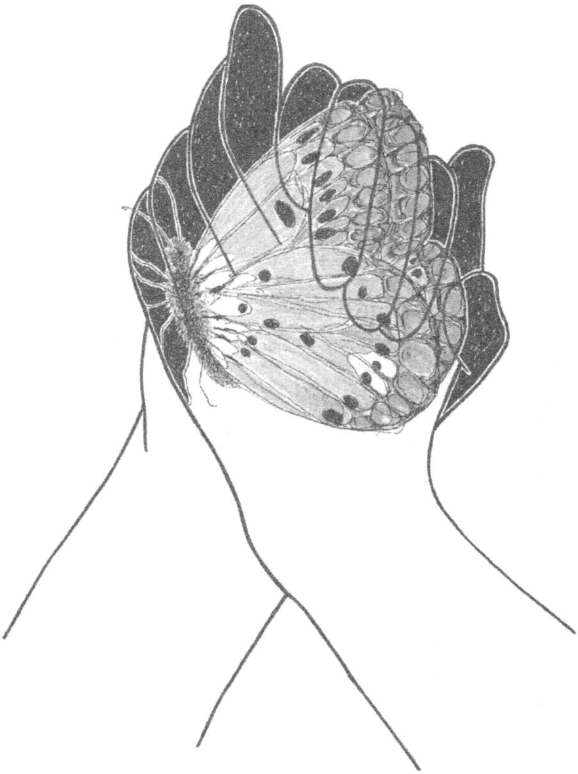

Cumbrian stars

these Cumbrian stars
have rested above your head
they illuminated your heart
and all as you restfully slept
in your Cumbrian bed

and in the delightful whiles
amongst the rain-soaked greens
your Cumbrian constellations
are turning steady and burning
whether seen or unseen

don't misperceive your Cumbrian soul
for its layers may go undiscovered
deep waters hold the greatest treasure
the watching stars that know you
are constantly astounded and enamoured

About the Author

Writing has featured in Catriona's life for many years. Her grandmother wrote poems and it also became a way of expressing herself for Catriona. It became an exploration of inner worlds: a safe place for self-expression and solace for such an introvert. She was sure that all the answers to her questions about life were hiding inside herself. Finding inspiration in the joy of nature, stillness and the discomfort of noise and busyness; realising it's all communication. Inspired by the stream of thoughts and feelings and the noticing which ones she wanted to follow and give life to.

Catriona joined a creative writing group in 2017 called Mungrisdale Writers. Other than writing poems for her children when they were young, this was the first time she shared her poems. Writing supported her greatly in her most challenging time: the passing of her 13-year-old daughter, and continues to do so.

Catriona fell in love with ink pens and drawing in her teens. Even though over the years she has experimented with many creative ideas, she is always drawn back to this first love. She grew up in Cumbria and continues to live there; happily surrounded by family, friends and pets, hills, trees, rivers and wildlife. A favourite pastime is being out and about with her Border terrier Miri.

Also by Catriona

…don't you think when we see heaven, we forget ourselves and return to oneness, even if it's just for a moment…

Printed in Great Britain
by Amazon

43171586R00091